A MESSAGE TO READERS

Welcome to the **Great Figures in History** series by **Y. kids**. These biographies of some of the world's most influential people will take you on an exciting journey through history. These are the stories of great scientists, leaders, artists, and inventors who have shaped the world we live in today.

How did these people make a difference in their world? You will see from their stories that things did not always come easily for them. Just like many of us, they often had problems in school or at home. Some of them had to overcome poverty and hardship. Still others faced discrimination because of their religion, gender, or the color of their skin. But all of these **Great Figures in History** worked tirelessly and succeeded despite many challenges.

Sing, an adventurer from Planet Mud, will be your guide through the lives of these famous historical figures. The people of Sing's planet are in great danger, facing a strange disease that drains their mental powers. To save the people of Planet Mud, Sing must travel through space and time and try to capture the mental powers of several **Great Figures in History**. Will Sing be successful in his journey? You will have to read to find out!

If you enjoy this story, visit our website, **www.myykids.com**, to see other books in the Great Figures in History series. You can also visit the website to let us know what you liked or didn't like about the book, or to leave suggestions for other stories you would like to see.

A NOTE TO PARENTS AND TEACHERS

Y. kids welcomes you to Educational Manga Comics. We certainly hope that your child or student will enjoy reading our books. The Educational Manga Comics present material in "manga" form, a comic story style developed in Japan that is enjoying enormous popularity with young people today. These books deliver substantial educational content in a fun and easy-to-follow visual format.

At the end of each book, you will find bonus features—including a historical timeline, a summary of the individual's enduring cultural significance, and a list of suggested Web and print resources for related information—to enhance your reader's learning experience. Our website, **www.myykids. com**, offers supplemental activities, resources, and study material to help you incorporate **Y. kids** books into your child's reading at home or into a classroom curriculum.

Our entire selection of Educational Manga Comics, covering math, science, history, biographies, and literature, is available on our website. The website also has a feedback option, and we welcome your input.

CONTENTS

WHO'S WHO?

Young Einstein

EINSTEIN

One of the world's greatest physicists. He contributed to the development of physics with his theory of relativity and quantum theory. He was also an anti-war activist and a pacifist.

MILEVA MARIC

Einstein's first wife. She went to college with Einstein and married him soon after. She was also a scientist. They had two sons together.

MARCEL GROSSMAN

Einstein's friend from college. He helped Einstein with homework in college, and helped Einstein find his first job.

ELSA EINSTEIN

Einstein's second wife. She nursed him when he was ill, and later married him. She supported Einstein through his later years.

Einstein's **PARENTS**

MICHELE BESSO
Einstein's friend.

AMY
Einstein's sister.

JACOB
Einstein's uncle.

The residents of Planet Mud in the Andromeda Galaxy have been suffering from a strange illness.

The Planet Mud Disease Control Committee has reported that this plague was caused by a so-called Confusion Virus that drains mental energy from people. Once affected by the virus, people suffer strange symptoms such as tiredness and frustration.

The Planet Mud Disease Control Committee has suggested a solution to this plague. They hope to clone aspects of the mental energy from some of the greatest souls of Planet Earth. When the Cam-cam records the lives of the great souls, it can collect copies of their unique and special mental energy. This mental energy is then refined into crystallized mental energy to be injected into the suffering residents of Planet Mud.

It is Sing's job to collect these crystallized fairies of each great soul's mental energy.

Sing An explorer from Planet Mud. He was dispatched by the Planet Mud Disease Control Committee to collect mental energies from the great souls of Planet Earth.

Alpha Plus Sing's assistant robot who keeps him out of trouble. His vast store of information can solve many questions during their adventures.

Cam-cam An invention from Planet Mud. When it records the lives of the great people, their mental energy is copied and refined.

Curiosity Fairy With the golden dust from this fairy, one's brain becomes more active, and one's curiosity and desire for knowledge increase. This intellectual power can lead to amazing discoveries or creations.

PROLOGUE

* Cam-cam: An energy collector specially manufactured by the GovLab of Planet Mud.

9

....

FINALLY, WE CAME UP WITH A SOLUTION. WE WILL COLLECT MENTAL ENERGY SAMPLES FROM SOME OF EARTH'S GREATEST PEOPLE, AND THEN INJECT THEM INTO OUR PATIENTS.

WE SHOULD NOT WASTE TIME LIKE THIS. LET'S HURRY UP AND FIND EINSTEIN AS SOON AS POSSIBLE.

HEY, YOU FOUND IT!

....

THIS IS A COMPASS NEEDLE, ISN'T IT? WHY IS IT ON THE FLOOR?

THE COMPASS WAS SO MARVELOUS, I HAD TO OPEN IT TO LOOK INSIDE, BUT THEN I DROPPED THE NEEDLE.

HMM. WHAT IS SO MARVELOUS ABOUT A COMPASS?

THEY SAY THE RED PART OF THE NEEDLE ALWAYS POINTS NORTH. I'M CURIOUS ABOUT HOW IT WORKS.

YOU KNOW WHY, DAD, DON'T YOU? PLEASE TELL ME, WON'T YOU?

OH, DEAR! OUR CURIOUS ALBERT IS ALWAYS ASKING QUESTIONS.

13

16

He grew up comfortably with his mother and father, who ran an electric appliance factory, his sister, Maja, and his uncle, Jacob.

Although brought up in an ordinary family, Einstein was no ordinary child.

He had an exceptionally strong sense of curiosity, and would focus on a question (sometimes forgetting to sleep) until he found an answer.

This strong curiosity was the driving force behind Einstein's growth into a great scientist.

IT IS HARD TO BELIEVE THAT JUST CURIOSITY HELPED EINSTEIN BECOME A GREAT SCIENTIST.

I WONDER HOW THIS SHY KID WILL DO IN SCHOOL.

COME ON, TIME MACHINE! LET'S GO TO EINSTEIN'S FUTURE!

SNAP   SNAP

BUT...
I WASN'T!
I WAS JUST CURIOUS.

GO TO THE OFFICE. NOW!

DID YOUR TEACHER SCOLD YOU AGAIN?

YES, DAD. I WILL DO AS YOU SAY.

YOU'RE A GOOD SON. CHEER UP.

Because the German education system was so rigid at the time, school was tough for Einstein, who liked to explore ideas completely.

Therefore, Einstein's school grades were always low, and his friends jeered at him, calling him dull-witted. His school days were frustrating and lonely.

EPISODE 2
MATH IS MY FRIEND

In 1889, when Einstein was 10 years old, he entered the Luitpold Gymnasium, a traditional German middle and high school.

WHEW. I'M SICK AND TIRED OF SCHOOL.

PAT

!

27

BUT THIS SCHOOL IS MUCH DIFFERENT FROM ELEMENTARY SCHOOL.

TEACHERS FORCE STUDENTS TO OBEY THEM WITHOUT QUESTION, LIKE SOLDIERS, AND FORCE US TO MEMORIZE EVERYTHING.

BUT I SHOULD GO TO SCHOOL ANYWAY, RIGHT?

THANK YOU FOR BRINGING MY PENCIL CASE. GOOD-BYE!

GERMANY IS BECOMING AS STRICT AS THE MILITARY. EVEN SCHOOLS HAVE BECOME THAT WAY···

At this time, Germany was led by Otto von Bismarck, nicknamed "The Iron Chancellor." He wanted to raise a great army to turn Germany into the most powerful nation in Europe. He demanded self-discipline and obedience from both soldiers and citizens. Even schools were run like an army.

Due to his experience in this kind of society, Einstein valued freedom for the rest of his life.

WHAT IF ALBERT LOSES INTEREST IN LEARNING?

HMM, IS THERE ANYTHING THAT CAN CHEER HIM UP? SOMETHING THAT CAN MOTIVATE HIM?

AH, I HAVE AN IDEA!

YES, THIS METHOD WILL WORK.

I'M BACK FROM SCHOOL.

WELCOME HOME. I WAS WAITING FOR YOU.

I HAVE SOMETHING TO SHOW YOU.

CAN WE TALK FOR A FEW MINUTES? PLEASE?

I'M SORRY, BUT I WANT TO BE ALONE.

SOMETHING HAPPENED AT SCHOOL AGAIN.

DID YOU RECEIVE YOUR GRADES TODAY?

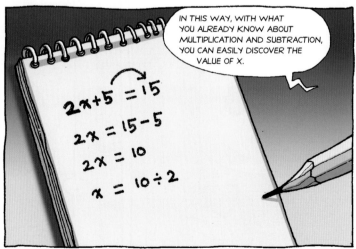

Einstein regained his interest in study thanks to the clever ideas of his uncle, Jacob. To Einstein, mathematics was an exciting friend to play with.

36

Once he started to solve a math problem, Einstein never gave up until he found the solution.

IF ONE SIDE IS X, AND THE OTHER SIDE IS · · ·

He sometimes even forgot to eat.

Please do not disturb! I am studying and will skip breakfast.

IT'S DINNER TIME, AND ALBERT IS STILL STUDYING IN HIS ROOM.

While learning mathematics, Einstein gradually developed an interest in science. He really liked the books *Power and Matter*, which contained information on the universe, and *Popular Natural Science*.

HUH · · · I CAN'T BELIEVE THIS.

HUH? THOSE ARE ALBERT'S SCIENCE AND MATHEMATICS TESTS, AREN'T THEY?

HE MUST HAVE CHEATED. HOW COULD SUCH A FOOLISH BOY GET SO HIGH A SCORE?

HE MAY NOT BE SUCH A FOOL. THIS IS THE HIGHEST SCORE IN THE CLASS.

For Einstein, who took no real interest in his classes, mathematics and science were more fun than anything.

However, the joy did not last for long. Einstein's life was about to change.

WE'VE DECIDED TO MOVE TO MILAN IN ITALY. YOUR DAD SAYS OUR FACTORY CANNOT SURVIVE IN MUNICH.

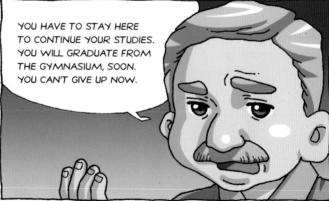

EPISODE 3
REUNITED WITH FAMILY

BROTHER, BE SURE TO COME TO MILAN AFTER GRADUATION.

Separation from his family, his only relief from the difficulties of school, was scary.

It was a painful experience for Einstein, who had no real friends.

Einstein tried hard to adapt to school life. It became impossible, though, as he had constant conflicts with his teachers and the persecution of the Jews grew worse.

YOU STINKING JEW, GO AWAY!

I CAN'T STAND IT ANYMORE.

WHAT IS THE USE IN GRADUATING FROM THIS HORRIBLE GYMNASIUM? I WOULD RATHER BE WITH MY FAMILY IN MILAN.

YOU WANT A MEDICAL EXCUSE?

NURSE

WHAT?

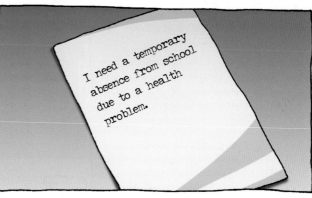

His family was sorry that Einstein had to stop his studies, but they greeted him happily because they knew how hard it had been for him to live alone.

Einstein spent a year enjoying the warm love of his family.

However, these happy days did not last long. An unexpected problem arose for Einstein.

A LETTER ARRIVED FOR YOU.

BUT YOU MUST GO. OTHERWISE, YOU WILL BE CONSIDERED A CRIMINAL AND BE PUT IN JAIL.

THEN···

....

I WILL GIVE UP MY GERMAN CITIZENSHIP.

I DON'T HAVE TO JOIN THE ARMY IF I AM NOT GERMAN.

WHAT ARE YOU SAYING? HOW WILL YOU BE ABLE TO LIVE, WITHOUT A COUNTRY?

NO, IT MIGHT BE A GOOD IDEA.

WHEN HE BECOMES AN ADULT, HE WILL BE ABLE TO BECOME A SWISS CITIZEN. SO HE WILL NOT HAVE ANY PROBLEM IF HE WAITS UNTIL THEN.

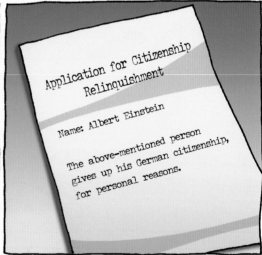

Application for Citizenship Relinquishment

Name: Albert Einstein

The above-mentioned person gives up his German citizenship, for personal reasons.

After giving up his German citizenship, Einstein lived without any formal citizenship until he turned 21 years old.

SO, IF YOU WON'T JOIN THE ARMY, WHAT ARE YOU GOING TO DO?

I WOULD LIKE TO BECOME AN ELECTRICAL ENGINEER LIKE YOU, DAD.

TO BECOME AN ELECTRICAL ENGINEER, YOU HAVE TO GRADUATE FROM COLLEGE.

BUT YOU NEED A GYMNASIUM DIPLOMA TO QUALIFY FOR COLLEGE. THAT IS THE PROBLEM.

In 1895, at the age of 16, Einstein went to Zurich, Switzerland, to take the entrance test. One month later, the results were announced.

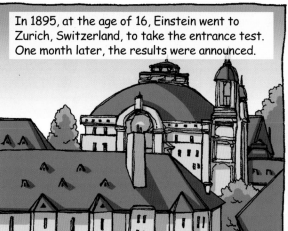

List of Accepted Students

Aldonito Lindberg

~~Albert Einstein~~

Anthony Schmidt

Anthony Taylon

I FAILED···

WE ARE LOOKING FOR ALBERT EINSTEIN.

HE LOOKS WORRIED. WHAT'S THE MATTER?

EINSTEIN HAS ALREADY LEFT THE SCHOOL.

I CAN'T HELP IT. I HAVE TO FIND OUT WHY EINSTEIN FAILED.

HUH? WHAT ARE YOU GOING TO DO?

SHH! QUICK, MAKE US LOOK LIKE HUMANS!

POP!

54

HE ALREADY WENT HOME...

THEN THERE SHOULD BE NO PROBLEM.

LET'S TELL HIM RIGHT AWAY!

DADADADA

EINSTEIN, WE'VE BROUGHT YOU SOME GOOD NEWS!

IS IT TRUE?

THIS IS GREAT!

EPISODE 4
CONGRATULATIONS, COLLEGE ENTRANTS!

I HAVE TO ATTEND A GYMNASIUM AGAIN. I'M SO TIRED OF SCHOOL.

KEEP YOUR CHIN UP, ALBERT. YOU ONLY NEED TO ENDURE IT FOR ONE MORE YEAR!

59

LET'S GO IN.

WELL, PROFESSOR···

I HAVE SOMETHING TO ASK YOU.

IS THIS GYMNASIUM SIMILAR TO THOSE IN GERMANY? FOR EXAMPLE, ARE THE RULES VERY STRICT··· OR···

HMM. GERMAN GYMNASIUMS ARE NOTORIOUS FOR BEING ROUGH.

YOU WILL HAVE TO WAIT TO SEE THINGS WITH YOUR OWN EYES, WON'T YOU?

62

SEE? ARE YOU RELIEVED NOW?

YES. IT'S REALLY NICE!

MR. WINTELER...

YOU SHOULDN'T ENCOURAGE STUDENTS TO BE ROWDY IN CLASS.

HAHA... I MUST HAVE FORGOTTEN. SORRY.

....

In Aarau's atmosphere of free learning, Einstein's grades finally improved.

He became more active and positive, and made new friends. Very quickly, the new Einstein became a leader among his peers.

However, one thing made Einstein more joyful than anything else…

LABORATORY

WOW, *THIS IS GREAT.*

The school had a physics laboratory full of equipment. Albert could test his hypotheses and theories with real experiments.

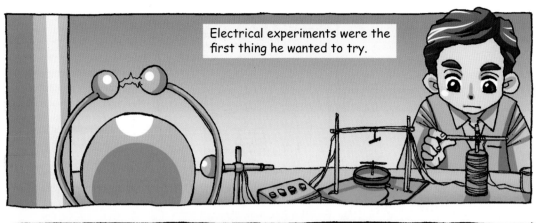

Electrical experiments were the first thing he wanted to try.

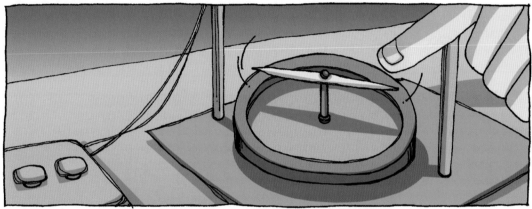

HMM··· IF LIGHT TRAVELS AS A WAVE, COULDN'T WE MATCH ITS SPEED, NO MATTER HOW FAST IT IS?

Einstein's study of this problem was the first step of his famous theory of relativity.

I WILL FIND THE ANSWER, NO MATTER WHAT!

YOU CAN DO IT, ALBERT!

While spending almost the whole year in the laboratory, Einstein gave up his dream of becoming an electrical engineer and began his career as a physicist.

HE IS STILL IN THE LABORATORY. HE REALLY IS DETERMINED.

I AM CERTAIN HE WILL BECOME A GREAT SCIENTIST.

One year later · · ·

ONE, TWO · · ·

THREE!

CONGRATULATIONS ON YOUR ADMISSION!

He entered the Swiss Federal Institute of Technology in Zurich without taking the entrance exam.

STUDY HARD AND BECOME A GREAT SCIENTIST.

I WILL. I WON'T LET YOU DOWN.

GOOD-BYE, FOR NOW.

EPISODE 5
TROUBLEMAKING COLLEGE STUDENT

YAWN!

IT'S TOO NICE OUTSIDE TO SIT IN CLASS.

ZZ...

LET'S BEGIN OUR MATH CLASS.

Swiss Federal Institute of Technology

LET ME CHECK ATTENDANCE FIRST.

Professor
Herman Minkofsky

MICHELLE BESSO.

HERE.

MARCEL GROSSMANN.

HERE.

ALBERT EINSTEIN.

....

....

....

ZZZZ

ALBERT, WAKE UP.

I STAYED UP ALL NIGHT DOING A PHYSICS EXPERIMENT. PLEASE LET ME REST DURING BREAK.

DUMMY, BREAK IS ALREADY OVER.

....

OH, NO!

I RESERVED A PHYSICS LABORATORY.

?

I HAVE TO GO FINISH MY EXPERIMENTS!

....!

IF YOU HAVE EYES, TAKE A LOOK AT THE ATTENDANCE BOOK.

YOU HAVE MISSED MORE CLASSES THAN YOU HAVE ATTENDED.

I KNOW YOUR MATH GRADES ARE THE BEST IN OUR SCHOOL.

....

BUT YOU CANNOT EXPECT TO LEARN IF YOU NEGLECT YOUR CLASSES.

Even at the Swiss Federal Institute of Technology, which was known for its excellent mathematics department, Einstein's math skills were the best of the best.

Because the mathematics professors had such high expectations for him, they were disappointed that Einstein was focused on physics rather than math.

OH, WELL…

DID YOU GET IN TROUBLE?

Marcel Grossmann and Michele Besso were close friends of Einstein. He only passed his classes with their help.

Heinrich Weber, head of the physics department

HIS EXPERIMENTS ARE NOT WRONG. ACTUALLY, THEY ARE EXCELLENT, ALMOST PERFECT.

HE COULD BE SUCH A GOOD STUDENT IF ONLY HE WOULD ATTEND HIS CLASSES.

THAT'S RIGHT.

WHY SHOULD WE BE SO TROUBLED BY ONE STUDENT?

Obviously, Einstein's habit of "studying in his own way" had not changed in college. He didn't attend classes that didn't interest him, and he wouldn't follow his professors' instructions. Again, his grades were not very good.

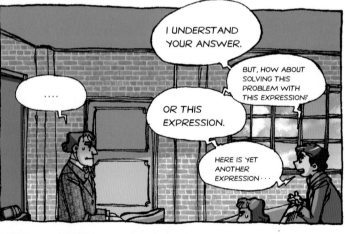

I UNDERSTAND YOUR ANSWER.

BUT, HOW ABOUT SOLVING THIS PROBLEM WITH THIS EXPRESSION?

....

OR THIS EXPRESSION.

HERE IS YET ANOTHER EXPRESSION...

MORE UNEXPECTED QUESTIONS?

78

His self-confidence, which was sometimes viewed as conceit, caused frequent disagreements with professors, especially Professor Weber.

EINSTEIN IS VERY SMART, BUT HE IS TOO PRESUMPTUOUS.

SUCH A FELLOW CAN NEVER BECOME A GREAT SCIENTIST!

When Einstein was a junior student, he got in trouble for his poor record of attendance.

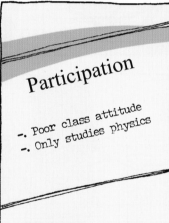

Participation

-. Poor class attitude
-. Only studies physics

However, Einstein did not take the criticisms seriously nor suffer from them.

He was happy just to be able to study physics to his heart's content.

WHAT EXPERIMENTS SHALL I DO TONIGHT?

But Einstein had one other concern. He was running short of money.

RIP

It was partly because his father's business failed, and also because he had to save money to officially become a Swiss Citizen. As a result, he never had enough money.

To earn money, Einstein worked as a private tutor in his spare time.

Even while studying and working, there was something Einstein never missed.

CAPE†

SORRY I'M LATE.

He met his friends for tea in a café once a week. This helped him stay peaceful, and it was fun to discuss ideas with his friends.

Mileva Maric, from Hungary, was a fellow physics student at Einstein's college.

She was an independent person and a very smart and eager scientist. Einstein was attracted by her brave attitude.

Although Mileva was shy and cautious, she opened her heart to the optimistic Einstein and quickly became friends with him.

They fell in love while working together in the laboratory, helping each other with their research.

At last, they promised to marry after graduation.

EPISODE 6
TROUBLES AND SUCCESS

The Swiss Federal Institute of Technology in Zurich, 1900

As a senior student, Einstein had to find a job for after graduation.

Most students wanted to become teachers, but Einstein wanted to keep researching physics at his college.

So he applied for the position of physics assistant instructor, to help the physics professor with research and grading.

DIRECTOR OF ADMINISTRATION

BUT, WHAT DO YOU MEAN?

DIRECTOR OF ADMINISTRATION

THE PROFESSORS HAVE DECIDED THAT WE COULD NOT GIVE YOU THE POSITION OF ASSISTANT INSTRUCTOR.

MY PHYSICS GRADES ARE THE BEST IN THE SCHOOL. I BELIEVE I AM QUALIFIED FOR THE POSITION. WHY CAN'T I HAVE THE JOB?

YOUR PHYSICS GRADES ARE CERTAINLY THE BEST, BUT YOUR GRADES FOR OTHER SUBJECTS ARE TOO LOW.

BUT THE PHYSICS GRADES ARE WHAT MATTER, RIGHT?

WELL …

BY ANY CHANCE...

...IS IT BECAUSE I'M JEWISH?

COUGH, COUGH

I DIDN'T REALIZE THAT SWITZERLAND WAS AS RACIST AS GERMANY.

FINE. I WILL FIND ANOTHER SCHOOL.

At the time, discrimination against Jews was growing more extreme in Europe. Jews were often denied jobs and housing, and in many countries they were forced to live in walled neighborhoods called ghettos.

Einstein could not accept his failure to become an assistant instructor, but there was nothing he could do about the school in Zurich.

He was faced with oppression and discrimination just for being Jewish.

But Einstein did not give up. He sent his resume to various colleges in Switzerland and Italy to find a position as an assistant instructor.

However, no schools wanted to hire a Jewish teacher.

Graduation day came while Einstein was still looking for a job.

Congratulations, Graduates of the Swiss Federal Institute of Technology!

Einstein, who seldom worried, grew impatient when he could not find a good job for two years after graduation.

NOW I CAN'T EVEN FIND TEACHER POSITIONS AT THE GYMNASIUM SCHOOLS, NOT TO MENTION ASSISTANT INSTRUCTOR POSITIONS.

MY MONEY WILL SOON RUN OUT···I FEEL SORRY FOR MILEVA.

OH, POOR EINSTEIN.

SWISS PATENT OFFICE

Einstein visited the director at the Patent Office in Bern, with a letter of recommendation from Grossmann's father.

YOUR SCIENCE GRADES ARE EXCELLENT. I WILL BE GLAD TO WORK WITH A TALENTED PERSON LIKE YOU.

WOW! I FINALLY GOT A JOB!

I SHOULD TELL MILEVA RIGHT AWAY.

Einstein was hired at the Swiss Patent Office in 1902.

The Swiss Patent Office examined new inventions and helped inventors create models of their inventions.

It was not an easy job to evaluate new technology and inventions, but Einstein was very good at his job.

As soon as Einstein had found financial stability, he married Mileva Maric in 1903.

In May 1904, their first son was born. They named him Hans.

He made a small group called 'Olympia Academy' with his friends. They enjoyed getting together to talk and discuss issues about science and philosophy.

Although Einstein was very busy working and taking care of his family, he still found time for his favorite thing.

WORK IS OVER.

HOW ABOUT GETTING A DRINK BEFORE GOING HOME?

GOOD! ALBERT, LET'S ALL GO.

HUH? WHERE IS HE?

HE'S NOT IN THE OFFICE. HE ALREADY WENT HOME.

DOES HE HAVE SOME SECRET TREASURE HIDDEN AT HOME? HE'S ALWAYS GOING HOME EARLY.

It was the experiment on light and time that he had been working on since his college days.

WELL, ISAAC NEWTON'S THEORIES MUST HAVE SOME ERRORS.

NEWTON SAID, "ALL THINGS MOVE BY ABSOLUTE PRINCIPLES." HOWEVER, THERE ARE NO ABSOLUTE PRINCIPLES.

A PERSON ON A SHIP LOOKS AS IF HE IS MOVING, FROM THE VIEWPOINT OF A PERSON STANDING ON THE DOCK. WHEREAS THE PERSON ON THE DOCK LOOKS AS IF HE IS THE ONE MOVING, FROM THE VIEWPOINT OF THE PERSON ON THE SHIP.

THIS MEANS THAT TIME AND SPACE ARE RELATIVE.

THEN, IF THE SPEED OF LIGHT IS FIXED AND THE FLOW OF TIME IS NOT FIXED, WHAT WOULD HAPPEN? PERHAPS, THE MASS OF MATTER WILL CHANGE···

I WON'T REST UNTIL I FIND THE ANSWER.

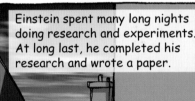

Einstein spent many long nights doing research and experiments. At long last, he completed his research and wrote a paper.

In 1905, Einstein published a paper that introduced the Theory of Special Relativity in the German science journal *Annalen der Physik*. His theory of special relativity argued, "When an object moves at the speed of light, either the length of the object decreases or its mass increases."

Annalen der Physik

University of Berlin, Germany

HUH? IT CAN'T BE TRUE!

Einstein's paper was confusing to many scientists, because special relativity challenged the theories of Newton, which were regarded as absolute truths in the world of physics.

WHAT KIND OF A THEORY IS THIS?

TIME ALWAYS FLOWS AT THE SAME SPEED. MASS DOES NOT CHANGE.

Before Einstein's theories were published, Newton's theories of motion were regarded as perfect, beyond the possibility of mistakes.

WHO PUBLISHED THIS THEORY?

HE IS ONLY 26 YEARS OLD.

WHAT? AN EMPLOYEE OF THE BERN PATENT OFFICE?

WHAT COULD AN EMPLOYEE OF THE PATENT OFFICE KNOW? HOW BOLD!

LET'S JUST IGNORE IT.

Einstein's theories were not accepted by professors and scientists at first; they were too revolutionary.

I SWEAR, THIS IS NOT AN ABSURDITY.

IF THE THEORY OF SPECIAL RELATIVITY IS PROVEN TO BE TRUE, IT WILL CHANGE PHYSICS FOREVER!

Doctor Franck, physics professor at the University of Berlin

I WILL TEST THIS NEW THEORY.

In 1906, a conference of physicists was held in Berlin. During this conference, Professor Franck presented the results of his own experiments.

Einstein's **Theory**

THESE RESULTS PROVE EINSTEIN'S THEORY OF SPECIAL RELATIVITY.

Einstein's **Theory**

THANKS TO THIS NEW THEORY FROM EINSTEIN, I REALIZED HOW MANY ERRORS THERE ARE IN OUR CURRENT UNDERSTANDING OF PHYSICS. WE MAY HAVE TO LEARN PHYSICS AGAIN, FROM SCRATCH.

THIS IS A GREAT DISCOVERY.

PERHAPS WE CAN SOON SOLVE THE MYSTERIES OF THE UNIVERSE.

To honor Einstein's great discovery, physicists called 1905 the "Miracle Year."

EINSTEIN IS SUCH A GREAT SCIENTIST!

I REALLY WANT TO MEET HIM.

MAY I ASK YOU SOMETHING?

I CAME TO MEET MR. EINSTEIN. WOULD YOU TELL ME WHERE HE IS?

WHAT'S THE OCCASION?

I WOULD LIKE TO HEAR ABOUT THE THEORY OF SPECIAL RELATIVITY HE PUBLISHED LAST YEAR.

PLEASE FOLLOW ME, THEN.

I CAME TO MEET MR. EINSTEIN.

SO, LET'S SIT HERE AND TALK. I AM EINSTEIN.

REALLY?

AH, YES.

I WAS JUST GOING HOME, SO WE HAVE SOME TIME. LET'S TALK.

HE IS REALLY KIND AND FRIENDLY.

IT'S SO NICE TO MEET YOU.

Even though Einstein became world famous, his attitude always remained humble.

THANK YOU SO MUCH FOR TALKING WITH ME.

Just as before, he lived an ordinary life, working at the patent office during the day and studying physics at home.

SHALL I GO HOME NOW?

IT'S DIFFICULT TO PUBLISH EVEN ONE PAPER IN A YEAR, BUT EINSTEIN PUBLISHED FIVE PAPERS IN 1906 AND SIX PAPERS IN 1907.

WELL, IF I TRIED, I COULD WRITE SUCH PAPERS, TOO.

PUHAHAHA

DID YOU JUST LAUGH AT ME?

ME? WHEN?

YOU MUST BE DEAF IF YOU DIDN'T HEAR IT! I CAN'T FORGIVE YOU!

SHH! YOUR VOICE IS TOO LOUD.

WHO WOULD HEAR OUR VOICES?

MAKE AS MUCH NOISE AS YOU LIKE. NO ONE CAN SEE US AS LONG AS WE HAVE OUR INVISIBILITY SYSTEM.

THWACK!

THAT'S STRANGE. IT FELT LIKE I SQUASHED SOMETHING.

HE DESERVED IT.

I'VE HAD ENOUGH OF THE LIBRARY FOR ONE DAY.

Einstein's busy research produced a series of new discoveries that surprised the whole world. Then in 1907, he announced a famous equation to simply explain the theory of special relativity.

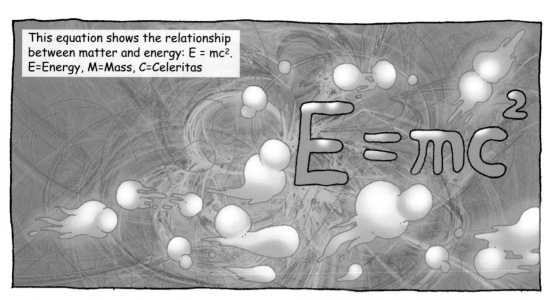

This equation shows the relationship between matter and energy: $E = mc^2$.
E=Energy, M=Mass, C=Celeritas

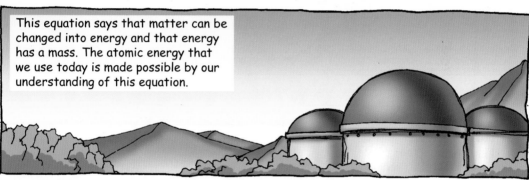

This equation says that matter can be changed into energy and that energy has a mass. The atomic energy that we use today is made possible by our understanding of this equation.

AMAZING.

THAT A MERE EMPLOYEE OF THE PATENT OFFICE SHOULD PUBLISH SUCH A REVOLUTIONARY PAPER···

The University of Zurich, 1908

IT IS ABSURD THAT SUCH A GREAT SCIENTIST SHOULD WORK AT A PATENT OFFICE. I WILL INVITE HIM TO OUR SCHOOL AS A PROFESSOR.

Professor Kleiner—a doctor of physics who liked Einstein's theory of special relativity

NOW, HOW SHALL WE SOLVE THIS PROBLEM?

At the time, Einstein had been working at the patent office during the day and teaching part-time in the evening at the University of Bern.

Although he wanted to become a college professor, he first had to build a career as a part-time instructor.

ALBERT, YOU HAVE A LETTER.

OH.

PROFESSORSHIP AT THE UNIVERSITY OF ZURICH!

WHY ARE YOU CRYING? YOU SHOULD BE HAPPY!

IS IT BAD NEWS?

NOT AT ALL. THIS IS AN INVITATION TO BE A PROFESSOR AT THE UNIVERSITY OF ZURICH.

109

THIS REMINDED ME OF MY EXPERIENCE OF TEN YEARS AGO.

I HAD SEARCHED THE WHOLE COUNTRY TO FIND A TEACHING JOB AT A COLLEGE, BUT NO SCHOOL ACCEPTED ME BECAUSE I WAS JEWISH.

HMM··· YOU MUST HAVE HAD MUCH TROUBLE.

?

BUT, MY FRIEND, IT WAS LONG AGO. NOW YOU SHOULD BE WALKING ON AIR WITH JOY.

CONGRATU-LATIONS!

I WILL BUY YOU DINNER! COME TO THE CAFÉ ACROSS THE STREET!

GREAT!

In October 1909, Einstein stopped working at the patent office, where he had been for the last seven years, and went to teach physics at the University of Zurich. He was just 30 years old.

Einstein's classes were very popular with students.

Other professors read from their notes during a class, which was boring.

Einstein encouraged his students to participate in solving problems.

Students respected Einstein and enjoyed talking with him about physics.

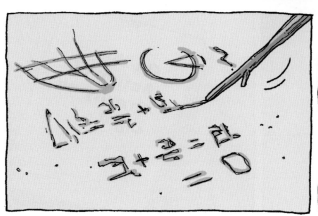

As Einstein's popularity grew, more and more universities wanted him. Several universities offered him teaching jobs.

HMM. I DON'T HAVE MUCH TIME FOR RESEARCH BECAUSE I AM SO BUSY TEACHING CLASSES. I SHOULD MOVE TO A SCHOOL THAT OFFERS ME MORE TIME FOR RESEARCH.

Einstein moved to the University of Prague (1911—1912) and then returned to the Swiss Federal Institute of Technology (1912—1913) in Zurich.

In 1911, he published another paper.

This paper explained the theory of special relativity in more depth, and claimed that light bends when it passes close to a source of high gravity, like our sun or any other star.

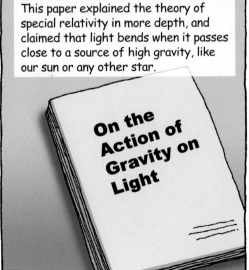

On the Action of Gravity on Light

The paper showed that gravity bends time and space.

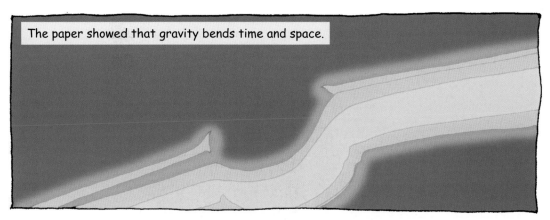

Einstein presented this paper at the Solvay Conference in Brussels, Belgium, and it attracted the attention of scientists from around the world.

However, this paper caused a lot of criticism. Many did not believe Einstein's theory.

RIDICULOUS! HOW CAN LIGHT BE BENT? IT IS AGAINST NEWTON'S LAW OF UNIVERSAL GRAVITATION.

IF EINSTEIN DOES NOT PROVIDE EVIDENCE, I WILL CHARGE HIM WITH FRAUD!

YES!

YOUR DECISION WAS WISE.

Einstein wanted to focus completely on his research to quiet his critics. So he made a big decision; he accepted an invitation from the government of Germany, which had an active physics research program.

After being away for twenty years, Einstein returned to Germany in 1914.

Einstein could research to his heart's content thanks to the support of the German government.

Two years later, in 1916, he published the *Theory of General Relativity*, which was an expansion of his earlier theory of special relativity.

HE FINALLY MANAGED TO SOLVE THE RELATIONSHIP OF GRAVITY TO TIME AND SPACE.

AMAZING.

HMM. THIS IS GREAT! BUT IT IS A PITY THAT THERE IS NO DETAILED EVIDENCE TO SUPPORT HIS IDEAS.

Arthur Eddington, a British astronomer

AS AN ASTRONOMER, I THINK I CAN PROVE HIS THEORY.

With the help of the British Royal Academy, Eddington visited Africa to witness the total eclipse of the sun on March 29, 1919.

Island of Principe, near the west coast of Africa

116

IT TURNED OUT TO BE TRUE AFTER ALL.

THE LIGHT IS BEING BENT BY GRAVITY!

DOCTOR EINSTEIN'S THEORY IS TRUE.

LONDON TIMES

Revolution of Physics, the Age of Relativity Theory Has Come!

When this news was spread by the newspapers, both physicists and common people became excited.

THIS IS ONE OF THE GREATEST ACHIEVEMENTS IN THE HISTORY OF HUMANKIND.

Doctor Thomson, chairman of the British Royal Academy

Everyone finally believed the theory of general relativity, and everywhere Einstein was the talk of the town.

Einstein's good fortune did not stop there.

In 1921, Einstein was awarded the Nobel Prize for Physics, the highest honor in physics.

Einstein's fame grew worldwide after he received the Nobel Prize.

He led a busy life, with requests for lectures coming from universities and institutes all over the world, including the United States and Great Britain.

THANK YOU FOR TAKING TIME OUT OF YOUR BUSY SCHEDULE TO ACCEPT OUR INTERVIEW.

YOU'RE WELCOME. I AM ALWAYS TRAVELING SOMEWHERE THESE DAYS.

WHAT DO YOU THINK?

LET'S BEGIN. SOME PEOPLE SAY THAT YOU HAVE SUCCEEDED AND BECOME FAMOUS JUST BECAUSE YOU ARE VERY LUCKY.

GROAN ...

WHY SHOULD WE RUN THE RISK? WHAT IF WE GET CAUGHT?

WE HAVE COME ALL THIS WAY, AND WE CANNOT RETURN WITHOUT MEETING EINSTEIN.

MANY PEOPLE SEEM TO THINK SO WHEN THEY SEE ME, NOW.

BUT I HAD MY SHARE OF PROBLEMS.

Before his fantastic discovery, Einstein had lived through two great trials.

BOOM

One of them was World War I.

During the war, the German government asked famous persons to publicly encourage the German people to support the war.

Einstein and others who hated war refused to publicly support the war.

PLEASE ANNOUNCE YOUR SUPPORT FOR THE WAR.

NO, I CANNOT.

ON THE CONTRARY, I WOULD LIKE TO ASK YOU TO STOP THE WAR AND WORK FOR PEACE.

WARS BRING ONLY DEATH AND DESTRUCTION.

EINSTEIN IS A TRAITOR WHO DOES NOT LOVE THE LAND OF HIS BIRTH!

THE JEWS SHOULD LEAVE GERMANY!

THERE IS NO PLACE FOR YOU HERE. YOU MUST LEAVE, AND QUICKLY!

The German government was angry with Einstein for not supporting the war, and encouraged people to harass him.

Fearing for his life, Einstein could not continue his research.

However, Einstein's troubles had begun even before he lived in Germany.

Einstein's home in Zurich, 1914

As World War I began, Einstein and his wife, Mileva, decided to divorce.

I DON'T WANT TO GO TO GERMANY.

123

AHH, MILEVA...

In the end, Einstein went to Germany alone. In 1919, after the war, he divorced Mileva and gave her custody of their two sons.

IT CAUSED ME A GREAT DEAL OF SADNESS, BUT I COULD ENDURE IT BY DEVOTING MYSELF TO STUDY.

THEN ARE YOU LIVING ALONE NOW?

NOT REALLY.

THERE YOU ARE! I'VE BEEN LOOKING FOR YOU, ALBERT.

ALLOW ME TO INTRODUCE MY WIFE.

DEAR ME! I DIDN'T KNOW YOU WERE HAVING AN INTERVIEW.

EXCUSE ME.

Her name was Elsa.
Einstein married her in 1919.

WOW, SHE IS BEAUTIFUL.

WHOOPS, MY TEA...

OUCH, IT'S HOT!

HAHA HAHA

HAHA HAHA

EPISODE 8
THE SCIENTIST WHO LOVED PEACE

Einstein rarely refused an invitation to lecture, and spent busy days traveling around the world.

He created and raised money for an antiwar fund and gave many speeches about peace.

One day, in 1933, he received some bad news while traveling to Belgium.

I HAVE BEEN EXPELLED FROM GERMANY? HOW CAN THIS BE?

WHAT ARE YOU TALKING ABOUT?

WHO MADE THIS DECISION?

IT WAS THE WORK OF THE NAZIS.

DOES HITLER REALLY WANT TO EXPEL ALL JEWS FROM GERMANY?

In 1933, the Nazis came into power in Germany and Adolf Hitler, the leader of the Nazi Party, became Chancellor of Germany.

He had hated the Jews since he was young and convinced the people to expel all Jews from Germany. Among them were many scientists, such as Einstein. The Nazis regarded Einstein as a particular problem because he led the peace movement.

So they not only denied his citizenship but also seized all his property, including his house. They offered a reward for anyone who caught him.

5 Millionen MK

Fortunately, Einstein was known all over the world, and he was invited to teach in the United States.

In the U.S. he worked as a full-time professor at Princeton University, while hoping for the downfall of Hitler and the Nazis.

1939

BOOM

Despite Einstein's wish, Hitler waged a war to try to conquer the world.

The German army rolled over Europe like a wave. Eventually, in 1940, even powerful France fell into their hands.

When Japan, an ally of Germany, attacked the U.S. at Pearl Harbor, the war developed into the Second World War. The flames of war spread from Europe to the whole world.

One day, Einstein received an unbelievable piece of news from fellow scientists who were also exiled from Germany.

IS IT TRUE?

HITLER IS DEVELOPING A URANIUM-BASED ATOMIC BOMB?

IT COULD BE COMPLETED SOON. WE MUST ACT QUICKLY.

Einstein was upset, because his theory of relativity was needed to create the atomic bomb.

Einstein wrote down his thoughts and sent a letter to Franklin Roosevelt, the American president.

GOOD HEAVENS, IS THIS TRUE?

The White House, 1939

PLEASE, SUMMON THE CABINET. THIS IS AN EMERGENCY!

Realizing the seriousness of the situation, President Roosevelt ordered the development of an atomic bomb. The atomic bomb was completed in 1945.

...

.....

However, the German army had already surrendered to the Allied Forces in May of that year, so fortunately the atomic bomb was not used on Germany.

A few days later, a second atomic bomb was dropped over Nagasaki.

As Einstein had feared, the atomic bomb was used at last. Imperial Japan, still at war with the U.S., was the first victim of an atomic attack. The city of Hiroshima was struck first.

With the surrender of Japan, the Second World War came to an end.

THE WAR IS OVER, BUT THE ATOMIC BOMB KILLED AS MANY AS 200,000 PEOPLE.

IT WAS DEVELOPED TO STOP THE NAZIS, BUT IT WAS I WHO SAID WE NEEDED IT.

EVEN THOUGH I DID NOT PERSONALLY DEVELOP IT, SCIENTISTS LIKE MYSELF CREATED THE BOMB.

SCIENTISTS SHOULD NOT USE THEIR KNOWLEDGE TO CREATE DEATH.

I CAN'T JUST SIT AND WATCH ANYMORE. I WON'T ALLOW SCIENCE TO BE MISUSED AS A THREAT TO WORLD PEACE.

After the use of the atomic bomb, Einstein worked even harder for world peace. He also urged his fellow scientists not to help develop weapons.

No War

Stop Making Weapons

No Atomic Bombs

No War

The movement to stop the development of atomic bombs spread throughout the whole world.

Stop Making Weapons

No War

No War

NO ATOMIC BOMBS

Einstein contributed to humankind as both a scientist and a leader of the world peace movement.

Always passionate and energetic, Einstein was now an old man with white hair, suffering from bad health.

After suffering from heart disease for some time, Einstein died in a hospital in Princeton, New Jersey, on April 18, 1955. He was 76 years old.

Every newspaper, TV, and radio station across the world reported on the death of Einstein. People lamented the death of such a great scientist and brave pacifist.

SHALL WE GO NOW?

OK, LET'S GO BACK.

DID YOU GATHER A SUFFICIENT SAMPLE OF HIS MENTAL ENERGY?

YES. NOW WE WILL GO HOME AND REFINE IT.

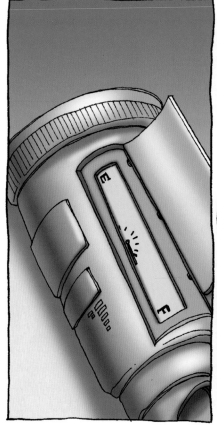

THE PEOPLE OF PLANET MUD ARE COUNTING ON US.

SUMMON OUR SPACESHIP.

YES, SIR!

136

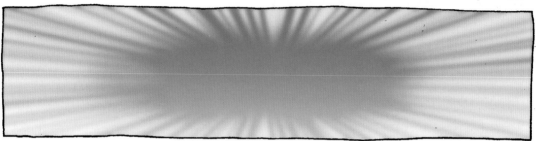

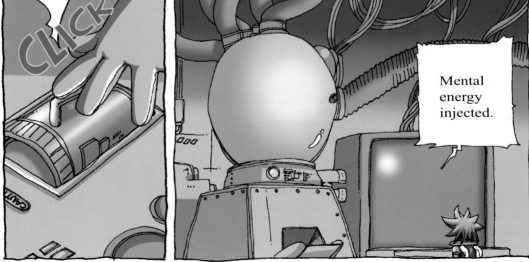

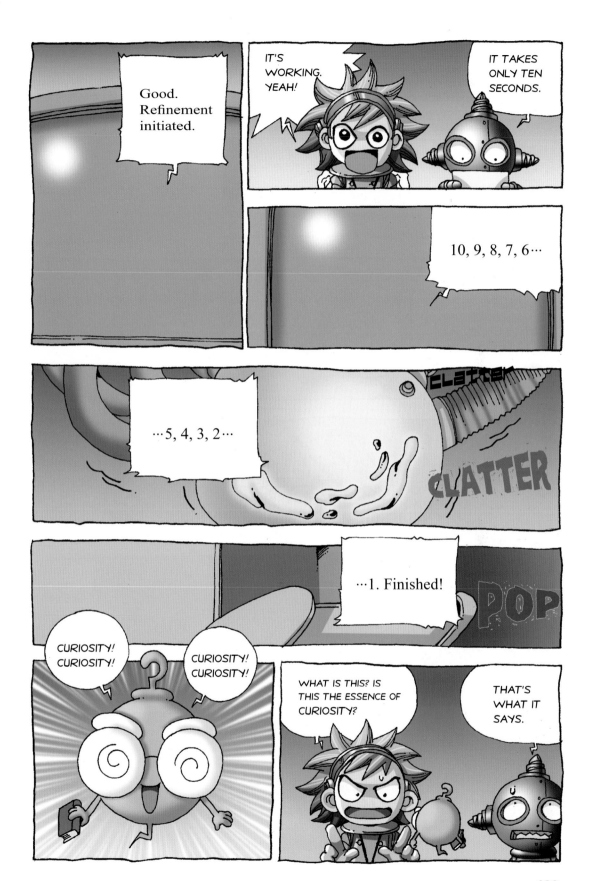

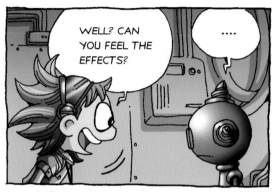

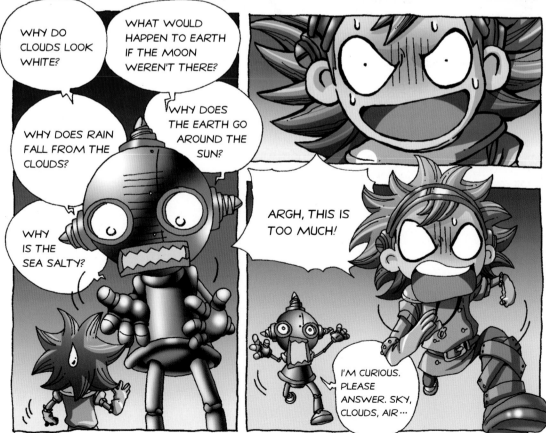

141

WHY IS EINSTEIN IMPORTANT?

Time magazine chose Albert Einstein as the Person of the Century. What makes Einstein's physics research so important?

- ❥ Einstein challenged Isaac Newton's 300-year-old theories about the universe, and made scientists reconsider all the laws of physics.

- ❥ He is most famous for his theory of special relativity. This theory says that time, weight, and mass are not constant, because when moving at high speeds, all of these things get compressed.

- ❥ Einstein's new ideas about relative time contributed to the modern time zones.

- ❥ The theory of relativity was used to develop nuclear power, as well as the atomic bomb.

- ❥ Einstein helped develop quantum mechanics. Though he spent his life looking for an even better, more complete theory, quantum mechanics has been used to produce transistors and lasers.

- ❥ Einstein provided the most accurate explanation of the universe's structure. His theory of general relativity is used by modern Global Positioning System (GPS) programs. Astronomers also use this theory to explain black holes in space.

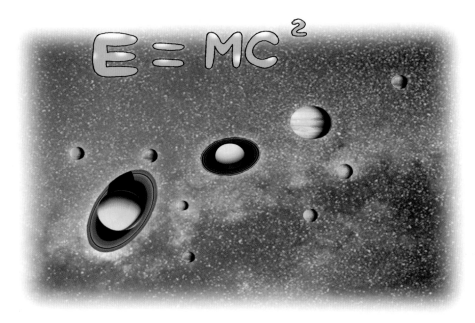

- The 99th element in the periodic table, discovered soon after his death, was named "einsteinium."

- Einstein created most of his groundbreaking theories with "thought experiments," rather than major lab experiments. Most of his ideas about gravity, light, and the universe couldn't even be tested until after his death!

 Fun Fact

Einstein's Brain

Because Einstein was a world-famous genius, many people were curious to know whether something was special about his brain. Einstein decided to let scientists study his brain after his death.

When Einstein died in 1955, Dr. Thomas Harvey of Princeton Hospital removed Einstein's brain. He cut the brain into 240 pieces. For 30 years, Einstein's brain was stored in two jars in a cardboard box at Dr. Harvey's house.

Over the years, Dr. Harvey gave some of the brain pieces to researchers. Since 1985, three research teams examined the weight, density, thickness, and texture of Einstein's brain. Each team found some unique characteristics of Einstein's brain, but every human has a unique brain. Although Einstein's brain may have been naturally good at mathematical reasoning, it was his strong personality, education, and curiosity that let him use his brain to become a great scientist. As Einstein said, "The important thing is not to stop questioning."

Where is Einstein's brain now? In 1996, Dr. Harvey returned the rest of the brain to scientists at Princeton Hospital, where Einstein died.

When	What
1870s–80s	**1879** Einstein is born **1880** Toilet paper is invented **1886** Coca-Cola is invented **1884** German chancellor Otto von Bismarck builds an empire in Africa **1889** The Eiffel Tower is completed
1890s	**1893** Chicago hosts the World's Fair **1893** The zipper is invented **1895** X-rays are discovered **1896** Famine occurs in India **1898** Marie Curie discovers radium **1898** The Spanish-American War begins
1900s	**1901** Walt Disney is born **1902** The teddy bear is created **1903** The Wright brothers take the first airplane flight **1905** Einstein publishes the theory of relativity **1908** Henry Ford sells the "Model T" **1909** Explorer Robert Peary reaches the North Pole
1910s	**1910** Thomas Edison makes the first "talkie" film **1912** The *Titanic* sinks **1914 –1919** World War I

When	What
1920s	**1921** The first robot is built **1922** Mussolini takes power in Italy **1922** Einstein is awarded the Nobel Prize in Physics for 1921 **1924** Stalin takes power in the Soviet Union **1928** Penicillin is discovered **1929** The stock market crash starts America's Great Depression
1930s	**1930** Pluto is discovered **1932** Amelia Earhart flies across the Atlantic **1932** James Chadwick discovers neutrons **1933** Hitler comes to power in Germany **1939–1945** World War II
1940s–50s	**1940** Churchill becomes Prime Minister of Great Britain **1943** The first computer is invented **1953** The Korean War ends **1953** DNA is discovered **1954** McDonald's is created

NAT.
MDCCC
XXX III
OB.
MDCCC
XCVI

ALFR
NOBEL

STILL CURIOUS ABOUT EINSTEIN?

On the Web

WAY TO GO, EINSTEIN

American Museum of Natural History
www.ology.amnh.org/einstein/
index.html

Discover Einstein's theories on light, space, and time with easy experiments, games, crafts, and projects.

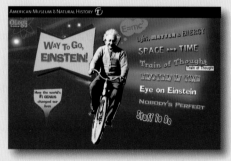

Courtesy of the American Musem of Natural History

THAT'S MY THEORY

PBS/Nova
www.pbs.org/wgbh/aso/mytheory/einstein/

Play this online game show to test your knowledge about Einstein and two other mystery scientists.

EINSTEIN'S BIG IDEA: TIME TRAVELER

PBS/Nova
www.pbs.org/wgbh/nova/einstein/hotsciencetwin/

How does time change as you travel through space? Find out when you send Captain Ein on an intergalactic journey in this interactive game.

TIME TRAVEL: THINK LIKE EINSTEIN

PBS/Nova
www.pbs.org/wgbh/nova/time/think.html

Quizzes and animations help you puzzle your way through Einstein's theory of relativity. Can you think like Einstein?

ALBERT EINSTEIN: EVERYTHING'S RELATIVE

The Why Files
http://whyfiles.org/052einstein/

Learn about Einstein's theories on the speed of light, black holes, and gravity, and how other scientists have tested Einstein's ideas.

At the Library

ASK ALBERT EINSTEIN

by Lynne Barasch (Farrar, Straus, & Giroux, 2005)

While teaching at Princeton, Einstein sometimes helped children learn arithmetic. In this picture book, two sisters write a letter to Einstein asking for help on their math homework.

ODD BOY OUT: YOUNG ALBERT EINSTEIN

by Don Brown (Houghton Mifflin, 2004)

Do you want to know what Einstein was like as a child? This picture book reveals Einstein as a fat baby, a little boy with a temper, and a budding scientist.

ALBERT EINSTEIN: PHYSICIST AND GENIUS

by Joyce Goldenstern (Enslow Publishers, 1995)

Who was Albert Einstein and why is he famous? Take a look at his scientific life and check out these five experiments and activities that will help you to understand his work and concepts.

RESCUING EINSTEIN'S COMPASS

by Shulamith Levey Oppenheim (Interlink, 2003)

Younger readers will enjoy this picture book about Theo's sailing trip with Einstein, where Theo learns the value of individual talents.

ASK UNCLE ALBERT

by Russell Stannard (Faber and Faber, 2005)

This book offers Einstein's answers to your trickiest science questions. For more in-depth studies of science questions, try the other books in Stannard's Uncle Albert series.

Y. kids

GREAT FIGURES IN HISTORY

ISBN: 978-981-054944-2
May 2007

ISBN: 978-981-054945-9
June 2007

ISBN: 978-981-054946-6
July 2007

ISBN: 978-981-057555-7
February 2008

ISBN: 978-981-057552-6
February 2008

ISBN: 978-981-057551-9
February 2008

MANGA LITERARY CLASSICS

ISBN: 978-981-054942-8
May 2007

ISBN: 978-981-054943-5
June 2007

ISBN: 978-981-054941-1
July 2007

ISBN: 978-981-057554-0
January 2008

ISBN: 978-981-057553-3
January 2008

ISBN: 978-981-057556-4
January 2008

EDUCATIONAL MANGA

ISBN: 981-05-2240-1

ISBN: 981-05-2241-X

ISBN: 981-05-2766-7

ISBN: 981-05-2765-9

ISBN: 981-05-2243-6

ISBN: 981-05-2238-X

ISBN: 981-05-2239-8

ISBN: 981-05-2768-3

ISBN: 981-005-2242-8

ISBN: 981-05-2767-5